Diego
from Madrid

Hello, I am Diego from Madrid! Come inside to meet my family and my friends...

Dulce Gamonal
Illustrated by Laurent Audouin

www.av2books.com

My name is Diego. I am eight years old. I live in Madrid, the capital of Spain. Madrid is a very big, busy city with beautiful streets like the Gran Vía and big squares like the Plaza Mayor. There are also amazing monuments that tourists love to photograph. Do you know about the Almudena Cathedral, or the Cibeles Fountain, or the Royal Palace of Zarzuela where the King and Queen live?

There are big museums in Madrid, like the Museo Nacional del Prado and the Reina Sofia National Art Center where you can see Picasso's famous painting, 'Guernica'. The city has a very big zoo too, with lots of wild animals, dolphins, bears and even pandas! Have you ever seen one?

Madrid

ZOO

My favorite place is El Retiro Park in the center of Madrid. You can roller skate, bike or even take a nap, and in the alleyways you can see lots of shows! I love to go canoeing with my dad and my friends in the big pool. And the Botanical Garden is close by, where you can see thousands of the world's plants and trees! Did you know that there are bonsai, cactuses and even carnivorous plants?

I live with my parents, my sister, Cristina, and my maternal grandmother in Lavapiés, a lively working class neighborhood in the city center. From our window you can see El Rastro, the flea market where on Sunday mornings you can find some real treasures! My mom says it's too noisy here, especially at night, but I love my neighborhood. There are people of all nationalities, and almost all my friends live here!

Coronas de la Almudena

Buñuelos

Hojaldres

10

My mom's name is Carmen and my dad's name is Diego, like me. They run a very traditional bakery. Everyone from the neighborhood comes to our place to eat "chocolate con churros", hot chocolate with donuts! They are a real delight, but my parents' real specialty is birthday cakes. They're always amazing and have fantastic decorations!

Every morning my friend, Manolo, picks me up and we walk to school together. Just about everywhere in Spain classes start at 9:00 a.m. and finish at 2:00 p.m. Then we go home for lunch. While my grandmother takes a nap, I do my homework. After a snack, I play soccer with Manolo and our friends! Then we have dinner around 9:30 p.m. This surprises a lot of people, but in Spain we eat dinner later than in other places in Europe. It's the Spanish rhythm.

13

Almost all my friends are in my class: Manolo, Youssef, Pedro, Eva, Juan... Our teacher, Almudena, makes us do a lot of art, and that's fine because it's my favorite subject! Last week, she took us to the Museo Nacional del Prado to see the paintings of Velázquez, one of the great Spanish painters. It was amazing. When we got back, we drew his famous painting, the 'Ladies in Waiting'. Can you see our drawings? They're all taped to the wall!

On Thursday afternoons I take lessons in Spanish guitar. It's also called classical guitar. Our teacher is really nice. He teaches us to play all sorts of tunes. Right now, we're practicing "bulerías" and "sévillanes" for the Flamenco show we're putting on in June. In the show, there's going to be a dancing boy and a dancing girl, a singer, and a "palmero" who'll accompany them by clapping his hands to the rhythm. You should come! It will be lots of fun!

My dad is a "hincha" of Real Madrid, one of the capital's soccer clubs. He often takes me to the Santiago Bernabéu Stadium to see the matches. It's an amazing place–a huge stadium with eight panoramic elevators. You even get to see the locker rooms, the trophy room and the dugout. On match days, sometimes there are more than 80,000 spectators in the stadium and the atmosphere is fantastic!

There are lots of festivals in Madrid! I love the San Isidro Festival in May. There's music, plays, bullfighting, a circus and the Gigantes y Cabezudos (Giants and Big Heads) parade! We dance the chotis in the traditional dress of chulapos and chulapas, to the music of street organs. At night, there's a spectacular fireworks display on the water over the Manzanares River that runs through Madrid. It's magical!

21

22

In all Spanish cities, there are bars where you can drink and eat
delicious tapas any time of the day or night. I love to sit at the counter
on the bar stools beside my dad and taste the delicious hams hanging
from the ceiling of the bar! You can eat lots of good food in Madrid:
cocido, made with chickpeas and meat, Spanish omelettes, garlic soup,
calamari sandwiches and paella.

23

LAS RAMBLAS

24

Over summer vacation, we go to visit my paternal grandparents who live in Barcelona. I love to walk around the Sagrada Familia cathedral with my family, and then go down to the flower and bird merchants on Las Ramblas. In the afternoons, we go swimming. Their house is only two metro stations from Barceloneta Beach. This beach is lined with palm trees and there's a sculpture of a twisted building that really makes me laugh!

For Christmas, my uncles, aunts and cousins come to our house in Madrid. We treat ourselves to loads of "turrones" and "polvorones" and we go to Mass. On St. Sylvester's Day, all Spaniards eat twelve grapes at the stroke of midnight. They say that brings good luck. And on January 6th, the Three Kings bring gifts to the children! The night before there's the "Cabalgata," the big parade with Melchior, Gaspar and Balthasar. It's always magical!

That's it! The tour is over!
I hope to see you soon
in Madrid. Goodbye!

Diego's Little Spanish-French-English Phrasebook

- **Hola!** Bonjour! Hello!
- **Me llamo Diego. ¿Y tú?** Je m'appelle Diego. Et toi ? My name is Diego. What's yours?
- **Tengo ocho años.** J'ai huit ans. I'm eight years old.
- **Vivo en Madrid.** J'habite à Madrid. I live in Madrid.
- **¿Y tú, dónde vives?** Et toi, où habites-tu ? Where do you live?
- **Mi abuela vive con nosotros.** Ma grand-mère habite avec nous. My grandmother lives with us.
- **¿Tienes hermanos y hermanas?** As-tu des frères et soeurs ? Do you have any brothers or sisters?
- **Me encanta comer jamón.** J'adore manger du jambon. I love ham.
- **Voy a clases de guitarra.** Je prends des cours de guitare. I take guitar lessons.
- **¿Te gusta el fútbol?** Aimes-tu le football ? Do you like football?
- **¡Las fiestas de San Isidro son muy divertidas!** Les fêtes de San Isidro sont très amusantes ! The San Isidro festival is so much fun!
- **¡Adiós! ¡Hasta luego!** Au revoir ! À bientôt ! Goodbye! See you soon!

- **Plaza Mayor**
the biggest
square in Madrid

- **polvorones**
short crust cookies

- **hincha**
soccer fan

- **turrón**
nougat

- **bulerías and sévillanes**
Andalusian songs

- **tortilla de patatas**
spanish potato
omelette, cooked
on both sides

- **tapas**
small cold or
hot plates that
are appetizers

- **chocolate con churros**
hot chocolate
with donuts

Your AV² Media Enhanced book gives you a fiction readalong online.
Log on to www.av2books.com and enter the unique book code from
page 2 to use your readalong.

AV² Readalong Navigation

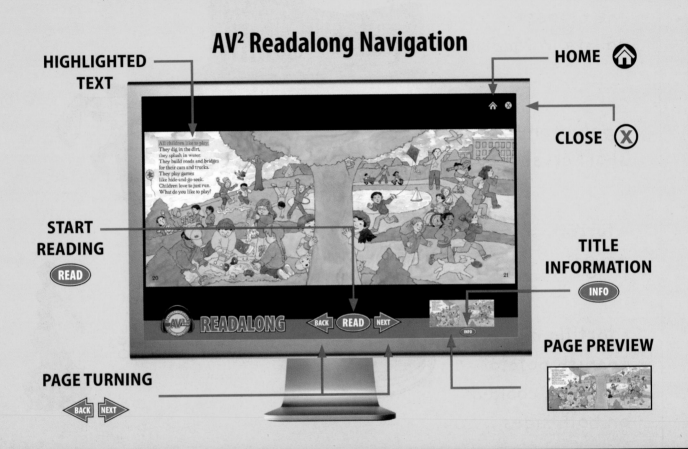

HIGHLIGHTED TEXT

HOME

CLOSE

START READING

READ

TITLE INFORMATION

INFO

PAGE TURNING

BACK NEXT

PAGE PREVIEW

Published by AV² by Weigl
350 5th Avenue, 59th Floor New York, NY 10118
Websites: www.av2books.com   www.weigl.com

Printed in the United States of America in North Mankato, Minnesota
1 2 3 4 5 6 7 8 9 0 18 17 16 15 14

042014
WEP080414

Library of Congress Control Number: 2014937136

ISBN 978-1-4896-2280-8 (hardcover)
ISBN 978-1-4896-2281-5 (single user eBook)
ISBN 978-1-4896-2282-2 (multi-user eBook)

Text copyright ©2012 by ABC MELODY.
Illustrations copyright ©2012 by ABC MELODY.
Published in 2012 by ABC MELODY.

ABC MELODY Éditions
26, rue Liancourt 75014
Paris, France